It is a great thing to start life
with a small number of really good books
which are your very own.
—Sir Arthur Conan Doyle

TALES OF MR. CINNAMON

by FRANCES B. WATTS
Illustrated by Marcia Mattingly

THE SATURDAY EVENING POST
Read-to-Me Series

THE CURTIS PUBLISHING COMPANY
Indianapolis, Indiana

THE CURTIS PUBLISHING COMPANY

Tales of Mr. Cinnamon

President, The Curtis Book Division: Jack Merritt
Managing Editor: Jacquelyn S. Sibert
Editor: Melinda A. Dunlevy
Assistant Editor: Amy L. Clark
Art Director/Designer: Jinny Sauer Hoffman
Technical Director: Greg Vanzo
Compositor: Patricia A. Stricker

Table of Contents

Mr. Cinnamon
Comes to Cozy Hollow

Cozy Hollow was a pretty little animal village. In the village was a pine-log schoolhouse, a village store, and a place called Hoppity Hall, where the animals held their parties, dances, and town meetings. And, as in all villages, there were lots of cottages and houses in Cozy Hollow, too.

Across the street from the village store stood a small home called Gingerbread Cottage. The cottage had been empty for a long time, and the Cozy Hollow folks kept hoping that someone would come to live in it.

Mr. Groundhog owned the village store, so he always hopped out of bed bright and early to get things ready for his customers. One brisk autumn morning when Mr. Groundhog was sweeping the store steps, he saw a most unusual sight. He spied a fuzzy, brown cinnamon bear in blue overalls coming up Main Street! The bear was pulling a big red wagon filled with tables, chairs, and lots of other furniture, and he was whistling as merrily as a bobolink.

Mr. Groundhog watched the bear pull his red wagon up to Gingerbread Cottage and start carrying the furniture through the cottage door. "Oho!" said Mr. Groundhog, dropping his broom. "Cozy Hollow has a newcomer! I'll have to go tell everybody!"

The groundhog waddled up and down the streets, knocking on everyone's door. "There's a cinnamon bear moving into Gingerbread Cottage!" he cried. "Come see!"

Soon Mr. Groundhog and a number of curious animals came running back to the village store. But across the street, there was no sign of the bear.

"Mr. Groundhog, are you certain that you saw this bear?" growled Mayor Possum. The mayor was feeling out of sorts because he had come off without eating his breakfast.

"Of course I saw him!" Mr. Groundhog replied.

Just then Miss Chipmunk, the schoolteacher, said, "Shhh! There he is! He's opening the door!"

The animals saw the bear come out of the front door carrying a sign on a post. He pounded the post into his front lawn, then went back into the cottage and closed the door.

"What does the sign say?" asked Mr. Poke-Turtle. "Read it to us, teacher."

Miss Chipmunk polished her glasses, then put them back on her nose. She read the sign aloud. It said:

MR. CINNAMON—INVENTOR AND
ODD-JOB BEAR

"He's an inventor!" exclaimed Granny Fox. "Fancy that!"

"And odd-job bear, too! That's fine!" said Mayor Possum. "Cozy Hollow needs someone who is helpful and handy!"

"I think we ought to do something to make him feel welcome," suggested Miss Chipmunk.

Then everybody began to talk at once, suggesting ways to welcome Mr. Cinnamon.

Finally, Mayor Possum said, "The best way to settle this is for me to appoint a Welcome Committee. The Welcome Committee will call on Mr. Cinnamon this afternoon."

Mayor Possum chose Miss Chipmunk, Mrs. Jump-Bunny, Doctor Raccoon, and himself as the Welcome Committee.

At four o'clock that afternoon the committee met at the village store. Everyone was dressed in his best clothes. Mayor Possum had polished his gold watch chain until it gleamed like a rope of stars. Miss Chipmunk had on a brand new hat trimmed with bittersweet berries.

They hurried over to Gingerbread Cottage and rang

8

the doorbell. Much to their surprise, the doorbell began to tinkle a little song "Come in, come in, whoever you are!" Then the door slowly opened by itself!

"My goodness!" squeaked Mrs. Jump-Bunny. "The door opened, but no one's in sight. Shall we go in?"

"We may as well," said Mayor Possum. "The doorbell is playing 'Come in, come in, whoever you are!' "

So they tiptoed into the cottage. Doctor Raccoon was the last one in line. Just as he was about to step inside, the door slammed shut with a bang!

"Who closed the door?" asked Miss Chipmunk. "Doctor Raccoon is still outside!" She tried to open the door again, but it wouldn't budge.

Just then Mr. Cinnamon came bouncing in from the kitchen. He was wearing an apron over his overalls, and there was a smudge of pink cake frosting on his nose. His round moonface was beaming with pleasure.

"Hello! Howdy there!" he cried. "I had a feeling someone might call today, so I've been baking Tasty Tea Cakes."

"Well, we're not all here yet," Mayor Possum spoke up. "The door closed. It won't open again, and Doctor Raccoon is still outside."

"Oh dear!" said Mr. Cinnamon. "I thought my *Friendly-door-opener* was such a nice, jolly invention. Now it doesn't work properly!"

The bear yanked and tugged at the doorknob. "There must be a screw loose somewhere," he sighed. "I'll go right out and fix it. Please sit down, folks, and make yourselves comfortable." Then Mr. Cinnamon raised the front window and climbed outside.

"What an *odd* character he is!" whispered Miss Chipmunk.

"Maybe that's why he calls himself an *odd-job* bear," Mrs. Jump-Bunny giggled.

"I don't think very highly of his inventions," muttered Mayor Possum. "Why does he have to have such a fancy door opener? Why can't he just *turn* the *knob* like everyone else?"

Now they could hear Mr. Cinnamon tapping the doorbell with his screwdriver. Pretty soon the bell began to play "Come in, come in, whoever you are!" and the door flew open. Doctor Raccoon stepped inside. He looked very cross at being left out for so long.

Suddenly, the door banged shut again. And now Mr. Cinnamon was left outside!

Mayor Possum ran to the window. "What shall we do now, Mr. Cinnamon?" he asked.

"Would you please climb out the window, Mayor Possum?" called the bear. "I'd like you to hold these screws for me while I use the screwdriver."

Mayor Possum wriggled out the window. He held the screws while Mr. Cinnamon drove them in. At last the doorbell played "Come in, come in, whoever you are!" and the door opened. Mr. Cinnamon scampered inside. But before Mayor Possum could get his foot on the step, the door banged shut again!

"Oh dear!" sighed Mrs. Jump-Bunny. "This sort of thing could go on all afternoon!"

"Yes," agreed Mr. Cinnamon. "We'd better pull Mayor Possum through the window, then have tea."

So they all began to hoist Mayor Possum through the

10

window. The mayor was very roly-poly, and he was quite a load to lift. Once, his watch chain caught on the window ledge. It took quite a while to untangle him, and that upset him a great deal. But finally, they got him inside again.

"Now," said the bear, "we'll all have some nice hot tea and Tasty Tea Cakes."

Mr. Cinnamon excused himself. Presently he invited his guests to come into the dining room. The dining room table was set for a tea party. In the middle of the table was a big, round tray filled with all sorts of frosted Tasty Tea Cakes.

"What lovely cakes!" remarked Mrs. Jump-Bunny, as they took their places.

"But just wait until you see my latest invention!" exclaimed Mr. Cinnamon. Then he took a key and began to wind a small mechanical spring in the center of the cake tray.

"Why are you winding the tray?" asked Doctor Raccoon.

"This tray is really a *Cake-go-round*," said Mr. Cinnamon. "It works like a little merry-go-round, you see. After I wind it up, it will slowly revolve. Then if you want a certain kind of cake, you don't have to reach and stretch for it. You just wait until the cake moves around in your direction."

"Wouldn't it be simpler just to *pass* the cakes?" asked Miss Chipmunk.

Mr. Cinnamon did not answer, for he had now finished winding his Cake-go-round. He smiled eagerly as he waited for his invention to start working. All at once it began to whirr and turn. Then it started to spin like a top. It spun faster and *faster* and FASTER!

"Oh dear!" cried Mr. Cinnamon. "Something has gone wrong! It's supposed to turn *slowly*!"

12

Now the Cake-go-round was spinning so fast that the Tasty Tea Cakes went whirling off the tray. Some of them flew around the room and landed frosting side down on the walls. One cake sailed past Mrs. Jump-Bunny, leaving a chocolate smudge on her ear. A cherry cake  smacked Doctor Raccoon on the nose. And a whipped-cream cake landed in the middle of Miss Chipmunk's new hat!

"For heaven's sake!" shouted Mayor Possum. "Turn that thing off!"

"I can't turn it off!" cried Mr. Cinnamon. "Hurry! Everybody duck under the table!"

Quickly everyone squeezed under the dining room table.

"The Cake-go-round will run down and stop by itself soon," Mr. Cinnamon assured them. "Oh, I'm so sorry my tea party turned out to be such a sticky one!"

"So am I," grumbled Miss Chipmunk. "My new hat is ruined!"

"Why do you invent things like Friendly-door-openers and Cake-go-rounds?" asked Doctor Raccoon. "Why don't you just open doors and pass cakes the way everyone else does?"

"I don't know," sighed the bear. "I guess it's because I have fun inventing nice, jolly things. I always keep hoping that other folks might enjoy them, too."

Pretty soon the whirring noise of the Cake-go-round stopped.

When all of them were out from under the table, they saw Tasty Tea Cakes sticking all over the walls, ceiling, and chandelier. But there were five cakes left on the Cake-go-round.

"Oh good!" cried Mr. Cinnamon. "Let's have tea. There are just enough cakes to go around!"

"I think the cakes have already been around!" Doctor Raccoon remarked dryly.

Then the animals all sat down and had three cups of tea and one Tasty Tea Cake apiece.

After tea, Mayor Possum said that it was time for them to leave.

"Thank you, Mr. Cinnamon," he said politely. "We had a very, er—er, interesting visit. And we all welcome you to Cozy Hollow."

"I love Cozy Hollow already," Mr. Cinnamon replied. "I

14

hope that you will find me to be a good, helpful, handy citizen."

Then the Welcome Committee climbed out the front window, because the Friendly-door-opener still wasn't working. They hurried over to the village store, where a lot of animals were waiting to hear about Mr. Cinnamon.

Mayor Possum told the folks all about the Welcome Committee's unusual visit. He told them about their strange experiences with the Friendly-door-opener and the Cake-go-round.

"My goodness!" chuckled Mr. Groundhog. "It looks as though Cozy Hollow has a lot of excitement in store. Mr. Cinnamon sounds like fun!"

"Come to think of it, he *is* fun," the mayor admitted. "You never quite know what he is going to do next!" Then Mayor Possum began to laugh.

Soon, everyone was laughing. As Miss Chipmunk wiped the whipped cream from her new hat, she laughed, too!

The Odd Job at the School

fter the Welcome Committee's visit, Mr. Cinnamon kept worrying about Miss Chipmunk's hat. He worried about it so much that he couldn't keep his mind on anything else. "Poor Miss Chipmunk," the sorry bear would sigh, "I can just imagine how upset she felt when that sticky Tasty Tea Cake landed on her new hat!"

One morning Mr. Cinnamon decided that he would do something nice for Miss Chipmunk so that she would know how sorry he was about her hat. He thought for a while, and soon he came up with a splendid idea.

Quickly Mr. Cinnamon ran behind Gingerbread Cottage and found his big red wagon. Then he hurried across the street to Mr. Groundhog's store.

"Good morning, Mr. Cinnamon," said Mr. Groundhog. "What may I do for you today?"

"I would like three cans of paint—yellow, blue, and red," said Mr. Cinnamon. "I'd also like a paintbrush, some turpentine, and a stepladder."

Mr. Groundhog said, "It looks as though you're going to do some painting."

"Yes," Mr. Cinnamon replied. "I feel sorry about Miss Chipmunk's hat, you see."

Mr. Groundhog *didn't* see at all, but he was too busy to ask questions. He sold Mr. Cinnamon the painting materials, then rushed away to dust his stockroom.

Then the bear put the things he had bought into his red wagon and trundled off to the pine-log schoolhouse. When he reached the school, he knocked on the door. Miss Chipmunk answered it. "Good morning," said the teacher.

"Howdy there, Miss Chipmunk," said Mr. Cinnamon. "You know, I'm an odd-job bear as well as an inventor. Today I'm going to do an odd job for you."

"Really?" replied Miss Chipmunk. "What sort of odd job?"

"I'm going to paint the schoolhouse roof," he told her.

"Well, that *would* be an *odd* job," Miss Chipmunk remarked. "The schoolhouse is made entirely of pine logs. No one ever paints pine logs. It isn't necessary."

"I know it's not *necessary*," said the bear. "But think how cheerful this drab schoolhouse will look with a nice bright roof!"

Mr. Cinnamon seemed so eager to do the job that Miss Chipmunk didn't have the heart to refuse him. She told him he could start painting right away.

"But be very quiet up there," she warned him. "The children are about to take a spelling test."

"What color would you like the roof?" he asked. "I have red, yellow, and blue paint."

"Red will do," Miss Chipmunk replied.

Whistling merrily, Mr. Cinnamon stirred the red paint, then climbed up to the gently sloping roof. It was breezy up there. Mr. Cinnamon took deep, joyous sniffs of the brisk fresh air. He looked out over the countryside and admired the crimson and gold colors of autumn. "Ah, it's good to be alive!" he yodeled at the top of his lungs. "IT'S GOOD TO BE ALIVE!"

Suddenly he heard Miss Chipmunk thumping on the schoolhouse ceiling with her pointer.

"Ooops!" said Mr. Cinnamon. "I forgot about the spelling test!"

The bear felt so upset about disturbing the children that he got all mixed up, and he started painting the roof backward. Instead of working from the peak of the roof out to the edges, he painted all the edges first and ended up on the peak.

When Mr. Cinnamon finished the job, there he was, backed up against the chimney, with wet paint all around him! "Oh dear!" he cried. "I can't go down without getting my feet all sticky. I'll just have to sit up here until the roof dries."

While Mr. Cinnamon sat waiting, he began to feel chilly. He started to shiver. He shivered until his teeth rattled. "I have an idea," he said. "I'll sit on top of the chimney! The warm smoke coming up from the schoolroom will keep me as toasty as a cinnamon bun." He was delighted with the joke

18

he had made. "Ho, ho," he chuckled softly, "Mr. Cinnamon will be as toasty as a cinnamon bun!"

Then he climbed up and sat on top of the chimney. Soon he felt warm again, and he was quite content to sit there enjoying the beauties of nature.

But down inside the school, Miss Chipmunk noticed that the room was growing very smoky. That was because Mr. Cinnamon was blocking the chimney flue. But of course Miss Chipmunk had no way of knowing that.

"Potpie Groundhog," she said, "please take a look at the stove. It seems to be acting up."

Little Potpie peeked into the stove. "I think it needs some more wood, Miss Chipmunk," he said. "The fire doesn't look very hot."

So Potpie tossed an armful of kindling wood on the fire

and pumped air into the stove with some big bellows. Soon the fire was roaring hot. Naturally, the smoke that went up the chimney was roaring hot too!

"Ouch!" yelled Mr. Cinnamon when he felt the hot air. "OUCH!"

He hopped off the chimney so fast that he kicked over

19

the can of red paint. The can rolled over and over. Mr. Cinnamon began to chase it.

All at once, he slipped on the slippery paint! The paint can rolled off the roof, and Mr. Cinnamon came tumbling down after it. And now there was a big, dripping blob of red paint on the side of the schoolhouse!

Miss Chipmunk heard the commotion and came running to the door. She found Mr. Cinnamon sitting in a puddle of paint. She also saw the big, red blob on the side of the schoolhouse.

"Oh dear!" she exclaimed. "How did this happen?"

"Well, I painted the roof backward by mistake," Mr. Cinnamon explained. "So I sat on the chimney while it dried. Then the chimney grew so hot that I hopped off and knocked over the paint. I slipped on the paint while I was chasing the paint can. And, well, here I am!"

"You *sat* on the *chimney*? No wonder my schoolroom was so smoky!" scolded Miss Chipmunk. "And now you have spilled all that red paint on the side of the schoolhouse!"

Mr. Cinnamon hung his head in shame. He had planned to do something nice for Miss Chipmunk because he had ruined her new hat. Now he had ruined her schoolhouse, too!

Just then, he had an idea. "Don't worry, Miss Chipmunk," he said. "I'll paint the sides of the schoolhouse *blue*. Then those red spots won't show."

"Very well," said Miss Chipmunk. "But be quiet about it. We're going to have singing class now."

Mr. Cinnamon stirred up the can of blue paint. Then he climbed up the stepladder and began to paint the sides of the schoolhouse. "Oh my," he sighed, feeling very sad, "I wonder if Miss Chipmunk will ever forgive me for all the trouble I've caused her?"

But Mr. Cinnamon could not be sad for long. The morning sun was shiny and cheerful. The fluttering autumn leaves reminded him of bright butterflies. And the songs of the singing class were so beautiful that his big heart swelled with joy.

Pretty soon Mr. Cinnamon began to sing along with the children. He joined them in singing "The Cozy Hollow Waltz," "The Froggie Serenade," and "Little Black Flies Love Pumpkin Pies." As he worked, he swung his paintbrush in time with the music.

Mr. Cinnamon kept painting until he was all finished except for one windowsill. Miss Chipmunk had opened the window to help clear the smoke out of the room.

"I'll have to be careful not to spill any paint inside the schoolroom," thought Mr. Cinnamon.

Now the children were singing "The Giggling Eagle." It was Mr. Cinnamon's favorite tune. So when he joined in, he sang with his whole heart and soul. He swayed from side to side on the ladder. He swung his paintbrush with wide, fancy flourishes.

Then suddenly, he lost his balance! Mr. Cinnamon and the can of blue paint went tumbling inside the window. The blue paint spattered the wall and the floor. And Mr. Cinnamon skidded down the third aisle, all the way down to Miss Chipmunk's desk!

"Why, hello, Mr. Cinnamon!" cried little Flossie Possum. "We were hoping you would drop in to see us before you went home!"

"But what a strange way to drop in!" giggled Jimmy Jump-Bunny.

Miss Chipmunk said, "Oh dear, Mr. Cinnamon! WHAT NEXT! Look at those blue paint spots all over the floor and wall!"

Mr. Cinnamon was so ashamed that his ears turned pink. Now he had caused Miss Chipmunk *more* trouble! "Please don't worry," he said. "The outside of the school is all finished, and I still have a can of yellow paint left. If I paint this room yellow, these blue spots won't show."

"Well, it should be done right away," said Miss Chipmunk. "But what shall I do with the children while you are in here painting?"

22

"You could give them a holiday," suggested Mr. Cinnamon helpfully.

"No, I couldn't do that," the teacher replied. "We have holidays only during Thanksgiving and Christmas vacations. It's a Cozy Hollow law."

"You could take them outside for a nice, long recess then," said Mr. Cinnamon.

"We certainly can't stay here while you paint," Miss Chipmunk said. "I guess we may as well have a long recess."

The teacher told the children to put on their wraps and find their lunch baskets. Then they all went outside.

The children spent a delightful day romping around in the crisp autumn air. They played Chase the Milkweed, Jump Over the Stump, and Acorn, Acorn, Who's Got the Acorn? While the children played, Miss Chipmunk sat on a tuft of moss and knitted socks for her friend, Granny Fox.

Meanwhile, Mr. Cinnamon moved the school desks into the coat closet. Then the bear painted the entire schoolroom. Much to his relief, he made no more mistakes and had no more accidents.

"There," cried Mr. Cinnamon, stepping outside, "I'm all finished!"

The children examined their school. The roof was as brilliant as a crimson leaf. The sides were a soft, summery blue. And the inside was as bright as spring sunshine.

"Isn't it *exciting*!" exclaimed Jimmy Jump-Bunny. "I bet we're the only animal village in the world with a red, yellow, and blue pine-log schoolhouse!"

"Yes, it's a very cheerful-looking school now," Miss Chipmunk agreed. "Thank you very much, Mr. Cinnamon."

Mr. Cinnamon was delighted that Miss Chipmunk liked his painting. He had planned to go right home and work on one of his inventions, but now he was so happy that he decided to stay and play some jolly games with the children.

Mr. Cinnamon and the children played Catch a Bear, Ride a Bear, and Tickle a Bear. Their laughter echoed all over Cozy Hollow.

"Oh, Miss Chipmunk," squealed Flossie Possum, "isn't Mr. Cinnamon nice?"

"He *is* nice," the teacher agreed, "but it's too bad that he does his odd jobs so *oddly*."

"I don't care," giggled Flossie. "I just *love* Mr. Cinnamon!"

"Yes," smiled Miss Chipmunk, "I guess we *all* love Mr. Cinnamon!"

The Fairy-Airy Popovers

ne morning Mr. Cinnamon glanced at the calendar and saw that it was Halloween. "Dear me! I almost forgot about the Halloween party at Hoppity Hall!" he said to himself. "I haven't the least notion what I will wear or what I will bake for my share of the refreshments!"

Right after breakfast, Mr. Cinnamon opened his cookbook and tried to find a recipe for something tasty to bake for the party. He saw recipes for apple dumplings, doughnuts, and devil's food cake. But he decided that they were too ordinary. "I'd like to make something *extra special*," he thought.

He leafed through the cookbook until he saw a recipe for popovers. "Yum, yum!" said the bear. "Granny used to make popovers. They were like crusty rolls, only they were

25

especially light because they were hollow in the center. I think I'll make a batch of popovers for the party!"

Mr. Cinnamon read the recipe. It called for flour, milk, eggs, salt, and melted butter. "It doesn't mention *baking powder*," he thought. "The popovers won't be light and airy without baking powder to make them rise. This cookbook is mistaken, I'm sure."

Humming a merry tune, the bear mixed the flour, milk, eggs, salt, and melted butter in his baking bowls. Then he added six spoonfuls of baking powder. It was some that he had invented himself, called *Doubly-bubbly baking powder.*

"There," said Mr. Cinnamon, as he tossed in the last spoonful, "I have been wanting to use this Doubly-bubbly baking powder ever since I invented it. I bet it will make these popovers as light and airy as balloons!"

Then Mr. Cinnamon poured the batter into muffin tins and popped them in the oven. He opened the windows so that the kitchen would not get too warm.

While the popovers were baking, Mr. Cinnamon decided to make his Halloween suit. "I'll put a sheet around myself and wear a pumpkin

26

over my head," he chuckled. "That will make a very unusual costume, because I'll be half ghost and half jack-o'-lantern."

Mr. Cinnamon scooped the seeds out of a big orange pumpkin. He cut two round eyes in it, a nose, and a big grinning mouth. Then he tried on his costume. He pinned a sheet around himself and put the pumpkin over his head. Then he looked into the mirror and laughed at his funny reflection.

Suddenly he smelled popovers! "Ooops!" he cried. "It's time for them to come out of the oven!" He tried to remove the pumpkin from his head. He pulled and tugged and twisted it, but the pumpkin stayed right where it was. "Oh well, I'll take the pumpkin off later," he said. "Right now I'd better see to the popovers."

Mr. Cinnamon opened the oven door. The popovers were a golden honey brown. They were the highest, lightest, airiest popovers he had ever seen! "Oh my, they're so beautiful! I'll have to give them a beautiful name," he thought. "I'll call them *Fairy-airy popovers*!"

Then he lifted them out of the oven. He loosened the popovers from the tins with a sharp knife. All of a sudden, the popovers rose right up into the air, as if they were on wings! "My goodness!" cried Mr. Cinnamon. "They really are *airy* popovers! I think my Doubly-bubbly baking powder is a little bit too bubbly!"

Now the popovers were drifting out the open window. "Oh, what shall I do!" he exclaimed. "My party refreshments are floating up Main Street! I'd better go capture them!"

Mr. Cinnamon remembered that there was an old butterfly net in the cellar. He found the butterfly net, then ran outdoors after his popovers. The bear was so excited that he forgot he still had on his Halloween costume. He galloped up Main Street in his white sheet and pumpkin head, swinging his butterfly net at the flyaway popovers. Now the popovers were rising higher and higher. Mr. Cinnamon leaped and jumped, but he could not manage to snare a single one!

Presently, Mrs. Jump-Bunny stepped out on her porch to sweep the steps. When she saw the weird pumpkin-headed creature, she almost fainted with fright. But keeping her wits about her, she tiptoed over to Mayor Possum's house.

"Oh, Mayor Possum," cried Mrs. Jump-Bunny, stumbling into the Possum parlor, "there's a terrible monster in Cozy Hollow! It's chasing queer little brown balloons with a butterfly net!"

Mayor Possum and his wife rushed outside behind Mrs. Jump-Bunny. By this time, other folks were gathering in the street.

"What is that gruesome thing, Mayor?" whispered Doctor Raccoon. "Do you suppose it's a creature from another world?"

"I don't know," the mayor replied. "Whatever it is, we shall have to capture it and lock it up!" Then he shouted, "March forward, everyone, and surround the enemy!"

The animals marched quickly forward and formed a tight circle around the pumpkin-headed figure, still leaping and swinging the butterfly net.

"Surrender, sir!" cried the mayor. "You are surrounded!"

"Oh, hello everybody!" said a familiar voice. "I'm having the worst time catching these Fairy-airy popovers!"

"Why, it's just Mr. Cinnamon!" said Mrs. Jump-Bunny. "We should have known that he's the only one in the world

29

who could cause such a commotion!"

Then Mr. Cinnamon remembered that he was dressed in his Halloween costume. "Oh my," he chuckled, "I must look very odd!"

"Yes, you do," scolded Mayor Possum. "You had us frightened out of our wits!"

"I'm sorry," said the bear. Then he explained how he had put Doubly-bubbly baking powder into his popovers and how they had floated out the window. "The reason I'm chasing them in my Halloween suit is that the pumpkin is stuck on my head," he added.

Everyone just had to laugh at Mr. Cinnamon's predicament. Then the animals looked up at the popovers. The little brown rolls were scattered all about now. Some were bobbling over the top of the blue plum tree. Some were floating above the village store. Another half dozen were sailing off toward Hoppity Hall.

"You'll have to wait until the popovers come down by themselves, Mr. Cinnamon," said Doctor Raccoon. "The moisture in the air will make them soggy sooner or later, then they will drop to earth."

"I guess I'll have to stir up another batch of popovers for the party then," sighed the bear.

"Never mind," said Mrs. Jump-Bunny hastily. "I'm making sweet-potato pies, and I'll bring an extra one for your share of the refreshments."

Mr. Cinnamon thanked the good bunny. Then, after Doctor Raccoon had removed the pumpkin from the bear's head, everyone went back to his own home.

At seven o'clock that evening, Mr. Cinnamon put on his

30

costume once more and hurried off to the Halloween party. When he opened the door of Hoppity Hall, he hardly recognized the place!

The hall was dark and shadowy, lighted only by a few flickering candles. The walls were lined with rustling, whispery cornstalks. Make-believe cobwebs and spiders dangled from the ceiling. Standing quietly around the room were goblins, witches, ghosts, and other strange masqueraders.

Mr. Cinnamon shivered. "My gracious, it's spooky in here," he whispered to a fierce old witch.

The witch was really Granny Fox. "Folks in Cozy Hollow love very spooky Halloween parties," Granny whispered back. "We try to make things as gruesome and scary as possible."

Suddenly a bloodcurdling scream echoed through the room, followed by a shrill ghostly wail!

"What's that!" cried Mr. Cinnamon.

"It's Mayor Possum," Granny Fox said. "He screams and wails now and then just to keep the Halloween party nice and spooky."

Pretty soon Mr. Groundhog, dressed as an old bat, began to play "The March of the Goblins and Ghouls" on his fiddle. Then the masqueraders stalked around the room in a weird and awesome parade. When the parade was over, everybody removed his mask.

Mr. Cinnamon discovered that the screech owl in front of him was really Mr. Poke-Turtle. "Howdy," said Mr. Cinnamon, "isn't this a fine, spooky party?"

"It's so-so," Mr. Poke-Turtle yawned. "We try, but somehow our parties never turn out to be spooky enough."

The animals then played a few scary games. They played Skeleton in the Closet, Cedar Hideaway, and Go Greet the Goblin.

Just before refreshments were served, Miss Chipmunk was asked to tell a ghost story. They snuffed out the candles and gathered around in a circle. In a low, quavery voice Miss Chipmunk began to tell about the ghost of the wild wolf from Blackfoot Hill. The ghost of the wild wolf had been seen on several Halloween nights in neighboring animal villages. It was said that the wolf once prowled around someone's rooftop in an attempt to slip down the chimney. The Cozy Hollow folks shuddered as Miss Chipmunk told the spine-chilling tale. Hoppity Hall was so quiet they could hear the cornstalks rustling against the walls.

Suddenly they heard a plopping noise upon the roof! PLOP!

"Shh! What was that?" squeaked Granny Fox.

Miss Chipmunk stopped talking.

PLOP. . .PLOP. . .PLOP. There it was again!

"It sounds as if someone is hopping over the roof!" squealed Mrs. Possum. "Do you suppose it's the ghost of the wild wolf from Blackfoot Hill?"

"Oh, we're afraid of ghosts!" shrieked the children.

"Now, now, don't be frightened," Mr. Cinnamon spoke up. "I'll go out and see who it is. If it's the ghost of the wild wolf, I'll tell him gently but firmly to go back to Blackfoot Hill."

"That's brave of you, Mr. Cinnamon," said Mayor Possum, "but we won't allow you to go out there alone. It would be dangerous!"

Everyone shivered with fright and wondered what to do. At last they all decided that Granny Fox should stay in Hoppity Hall with the children, and the rest of them would go outside with Mr. Cinnamon.

Slowly the animals tiptoed out the door. Some of them carried lanterns, because the night was as black as pitch.

"I'll climb up the drainpipe," Mr. Cinnamon whispered. "If I see the ghost of the wild wolf, I'll slide back down. Then we'll decide how we can get him to leave."

Slinging a lantern over his arm, Mr. Cinnamon climbed up the drainpipe. When the brave bear reached the edge of the roof, he cautiously held up the lantern and looked about.

"Well, well, well!" he remarked. Then he slid back down.

"What did you see?" asked the others. "Was it the ghost of the wild wolf?"

"No, it wasn't the ghost," answered Mr. Cinnamon.

"Well, what did you see then?" the animals clamored.

Mr. Cinnamon looked very sheepish. He hung his head. "I saw four soggy Fairy-airy popovers. The plops that we heard were simply my popovers dropping on the roof."

Everyone was so relieved that it was not the ghost that they all began to laugh. They laughed and laughed. Since no one seemed angry about the popovers, Mr. Cinnamon laughed loudest of all.

Then the folks went back inside for refreshments. They had apple juice, crullers, nut-chews, and sweet-potato pie.

Later, when they were leaving for home, Mayor Possum said, "Thanks to Mr. Cinnamon's Fairy-airy popovers, this has been the spookiest Halloween party ever held in Cozy Hollow!"

"That is what made the party such a big success," Miss Chipmunk remarked. "Halloween is supposed to be spooky."

Mr. Cinnamon whistled all the way home, because his Fairy-airy popovers had given everyone such a delightfully spooky time!

A Present
for Mr. Poke-Turtle

ne afternoon Mr. Cinnamon set out to rake Mrs. Jump-Bunny's yard. On the way he met Mr. Poke-Turtle, who was mending his front gate. "Howdy," said Mr. Cinnamon. "This is a nice, cool, nippy day, isn't it?"

Mr. Poke-Turtle nodded. "I've ordered a pair of pink earmuffs from the mail-order catalog," he said, "and I'm going to give them to Granny Fox. Her poor old ears get so chilly these days."

"Why, that's very thoughtful of you," said Mr. Cinnamon. He was about to move on when he spied a big, brown hare strutting up Main Street. The hare was wearing a loud

35

checkered vest and a fedora hat cocked over one eye.

"Say, who's that?" asked Mr. Cinnamon.

"Oh dear!" groaned Mr. Poke-Turtle. "That's Hooligan Hare from Cricket Crossing! Oh, I hate it when that hare comes to Cozy Hollow. He just loves to torment me!"

Pretty soon the hare reached the gate. "Hi, slowpoke," he said to the turtle. "How's my old poky pal today?"

"I'm no pal of *yours*," grumbled Mr. Poke-Turtle.

The hare laughed and tweaked the old turtle's nose. "Hey, slowpoke, when are you going to race with me?" he jeered.

Mr. Cinnamon could see that Hooligan Hare was a bully and a tease. "Mr. Hare," he said sternly, "if you don't stop bullying my friend, I'm afraid I shall have to spank you."

Hooligan Hare wiggled his nose in a very impudent manner. "I'm not bullying old slowpoke," he replied. "For years I've been begging him to run a race with me, but he's afraid to. He knows that I'll beat him, that's why."

Mr. Poke-Turtle blushed with embarrassment.

"See, it's true! Slowpoke *is* afraid to race with me," Hooligan boasted.

36

Suddenly a crowd of indignant Cozy Hollow folks came hurrying up the street. They all began to shout at the hare.

"Hooligan Hare," called Mayor Possum, "we've warned you to stop tormenting Mr. Poke-Turtle! I want you to leave Cozy Hollow at once, or I'll lock you up in Hoppity Hall!"

"All right, I'm leaving," whined the hare. "It's a waste of time to talk with this scaredy-cat turtle anyhow." Then Hooligan wiggled his impudent nose and hopped off toward Spruce Gum Road.

Mr. Poke-Turtle thanked Mayor Possum for ordering the hare out of town. After the other animals had gone, Mr. Cinnamon stayed on to chat for a moment.

"I wouldn't pay any attention to that hare, Mr. Poke-Turtle," said the kind bear. "You're not a scaredy-cat at all."

"But I *am* slow," sighed the turtle. "Oh, I'm poky all right. Wherever I go, I'm always late. Believe me, Mr. Cinnamon, it's a great trial to be slow."

"Yes, I imagine it is," Mr. Cinnamon agreed. Just then, he remembered the work he had to do. So the bear excused himself and went off to rake leaves for Mrs. Jump-Bunny.

While Mr. Cinnamon raked the leaves, he worried about Mr. Poke-Turtle. He grew sadder and sadder. "I'd certainly like to help that poor turtle," he thought. "I wish there was some way he could be speeded up a bit."

All at once Mr. Cinnamon began to hop with excitement. "I have an idea for an invention!" he cried. "If it works, Mr. Poke-Turtle will be the speediest turtle in the world!"

That very next morning the bear went into his workshop and started working on his invention. At the end of two weeks, it was all finished. The invention was a little open-air car, exactly the right size for a turtle. The car was painted red, and the wheels were bright yellow. Attached to it was a roomy sidecar for passengers. The little machine also had a merry horn that tooted "Hey-diddle-dum, here I come!"

Right away, Mr. Cinnamon hurried to Mr. Poke-Turtle's house. "Come on over!" he cried. "I have a present for you!"

When the turtle saw his present parked in Mr. Cinnamon's backyard, he blinked and said, "Well, well, what's this?"

"It's my latest invention, a *Turtlemobile!*" said Mr. Cinnamon. "When you want to go somewhere in a hurry, all you have to do is drive this."

"Will this Turtlemobile get me to parties and dances on time?" asked Mr. Poke-Turtle.

"Yes indeed," the bear assured him. "But you'll have to keep the tank full of red-hot pepper juice. Red-hot pepper juice is what makes it go, you see. And you must keep your foot on this pepper-juice pedal to keep it running."

"My, my!" the turtle chuckled. "This is some present! Thank you very much."

Then Mr. Cinnamon tried to teach Mr. Poke-Turtle how to drive his present. He showed him how to push the "start" and "stop" buttons. He told him to press his foot on the pepper-juice pedal when he wished to go faster.

But alas, the turtle learned very slowly. Besides that, he was a timid driver. He kept poking his head down into his shell when he felt that he was going too fast. Then the Turtlemobile would skid into Mr. Cinnamon's rosebushes.

"You mustn't be afraid of it, friend," Mr. Cinnamon told him. "Just don't lose your head, and you'll be all right."

"I never lose my head," said Mr. Poke-Turtle. "I just tuck

38

it away for safety."

At last it grew dark. Mr. Poke-Turtle was still very timid about driving. So Mr. Cinnamon pushed him home in the Turtlemobile.

"Now Mr. Poke-Turtle, you shouldn't give up," said the bear. "Tomorrow you ought to drive to the store when you do your marketing."

"I'm still leery of it," sighed the turtle, "but I'll try."

Early the next morning, Mr. Cinnamon went over to the store and sat down on the steps. Soon Mayor and Mrs. Possum, Doctor Raccoon, and a number of other customers arrived. Suddenly, everyone heard a loud putt-putt noise and the shrill screeching of wheels. Then Mr. Poke-Turtle came whizzing around the corner in his Turtlemobile! He zig-zagged wildly up Main Street, looking rather like a scatter-brained beetle. His green derby hat sailed into the ditch!

The ladies screamed and hid their eyes.

"Heavenly days!" cried Mayor Possum. "What's that ?"

"It's a Turtlemobile, my latest invention," Mr. Cinnamon explained. "But, mercy me, that turtle is driving too fast!

"Slow down, Mr. Poke-Turtle!" he shouted. "Take your foot off the pepper-juice pedal!"

Mr. Poke-Turtle was so confused that he pressed his foot *down* on the pedal. Then he went faster than ever!

"No, no!" cried the bear. "Hurry and push the 'stop' button!"

Mr. Poke-Turtle pushed what he thought was the "stop" button. But he pushed the horn by mistake. The horn tooted "Hey-diddle-dum, here I come!" The noise frightened the turtle, and he quickly poked his head into his shell. Then he couldn't see where he was going.

"Oh, look!" squealed Mrs. Possum. "He's going to bump into the blue plum tree!"

Sure enough, the Turtlemobile hit the blue plum tree with a walloping thud!

Everyone ran over to the tree. Mr. Cinnamon peered down into the turtle's shell. "Is everything all right?" he asked.

"I guess so," the turtle answered.

"Well, thank goodness!" said Doctor Raccoon. "Mr. Cinnamon, you should be ashamed of yourself for inventing such a dangerous vehicle!"

"But it's not dangerous," Mr. Cinnamon replied. "The turtle just lost his head."

40

Slowly Mr. Poke-Turtle pushed his head out of his shell. "No, I didn't lose my head," he said. "It's right here. But I know one thing. I'll never get used to this speedy car. It makes me far too nervous."

"I thought you were tired of being *slow*," said Mr. Cinnamon. "That's the reason I invented the Turtlemobile."

"Well, it was a grave mistake to invent it," Mayor Possum spoke up. "We can't have turtles zigzagging around Cozy Hollow like this. It's too upsetting. Today he almost knocked down our blue plum tree. The next time, something worse may happen."

Some of the other animals scolded Mr. Cinnamon, too. They also insisted that Mr. Poke-Turtle keep his present in his yard, and they told him not to drive it again. The turtle readily agreed. Mr. Cinnamon was very sorry that his invention had been such a failure. He was sure that Mr. Poke-Turtle might like his car if only he were not afraid of it.

Within a few days, the Turtlemobile was all but forgotten. Cold weather was beginning to set in. The animals were kept busy chopping and stacking wood for the long winter ahead.

One morning when Mr. Cinnamon went by Mr. Poke-Turtle's house, he found the turtle chatting with Granny Fox beside the gate. Granny was wearing the pink earmuffs that Mr. Poke-Turtle had given her.

"How do you like my new earmuffs?" she asked Mr. Cinnamon. "They make my ears feel as warm as toasted chestnuts."

"They're dandy earmuffs, Granny," smiled Mr. Cinnamon.

Just then, who should come swaggering up the street but Hooligan Hare from Cricket Crossing!

"Fiddlesticks!" groaned Mr. Poke-Turtle. "Here comes that boastful hare again. Oh, I'd give anything if I could beat him in a race. But he can run a mile while I'm running a yard. That's the whole trouble."

"Hi, slowpoke," jeered the hare, "how about a race?" Then he turned his attention to Granny Fox. "Those are mighty pretty earmuffs you're wearing," he said. With a wicked laugh, he snatched the earmuffs from Granny's ears and went leaping off toward Spruce Gum Road.

"Thanks for the present, Granny!" he hooted with glee.

"Let's go after him!" cried Mr. Cinnamon. "He shouldn't be allowed to treat folks that way!"

By this time, other animals had gathered around. "There's no use trying to catch him," said Mayor Possum. "Hooligan's the fastest hare in the county."

Then suddenly, Mr. Poke-Turtle came chugging out of his yard in his Turtlemobile. "I'm going after Granny's earmuffs!" he shouted. "A turtle can't beat Hooligan Hare. But maybe a turtle in a Turtlemobile can!"

"You may need help! I'll go with you!" cried Mr. Cinnamon. Quickly the bear hopped into the sidecar.

The ride down Spruce Gum Road was a wild one indeed! Mr. Poke-Turtle was so upset and nervous that he could hardly steer. He kept zigzagging over the road, hitting all the bumps. Mr. Cinnamon was bounced out of the sidecar twice and had to run to catch up.

"Don't lose your head, Mr. Poke-Turtle!" cried the bear. "If you'll just stay calm we'll catch Hooligan Hare in no time."

Mr. Cinnamon's encouraging words calmed the turtle

42

down. After that, he drove in a straight path and missed most of the bumps.

Pretty soon they spied Hooligan Hare around a bend in the road! He was just skipping along in Granny's earmuffs.

The hare glanced behind him. His eyes popped with astonishment when he saw the red Turtlemobile.

Mr. Poke-Turtle blew the horn. "HEY-DIDDLE-DUM, HERE I COME!"

Hooligan Hare ran as fast as he could run!

"Step on the pepper-juice pedal!" called Mr. Cinnamon.

Mr. Poke-Turtle stepped on the pedal. The Turtlemobile shot forward like a ball of red fire. Soon it was right on the heels of the hare. "Move over, Hooligan, or I'll bump you into the ditch!" shouted the turtle. "This is one race you're not going to win!"

Quickly the hare leaped to the side of the road. The Turtlemobile zoomed past him, then jerked to a stop.

"Now, give me those earmuffs, Hooligan!" ordered Mr. Poke-Turtle.

Hooligan was so stunned at having lost a race with a turtle that he handed over the earmuffs without a word. Then,

43

muttering gloomily, he limped toward Cricket Crossing.

Mr. Cinnamon and Mr. Poke-Turtle laughed and sang all the way home. When they drove into Cozy Hollow, the animals were waiting for them at the village store. Triumphantly, Mr. Cinnamon waved Granny's earmuffs!

"Hurrah!" the animals shouted. "Hurrah!" It was a proud day for the little village. Cozy Hollow's own Mr. Poke-Turtle had won a race with the fastest hare in the county!

But Mr. Cinnamon was the real hero of the day, because his Turtlemobile had made it all possible. The animals lifted the bear onto their shoulders and carried him down Main Street.

That night a dance was held at Hoppity Hall to celebrate the victory. Granny Fox was so pleased to have her pink earmuffs back again that she wore them all evening. And Mr. Poke-Turtle was the first one to arrive at the dance, because he drove to Hoppity Hall in his Turtlemobile!

The Christmas Program

One evening the Cozy Hollow folks had an important meeting at Hoppity Hall. At the meeting they were going to decide what they would do for their annual Christmas celebration.

Mayor Possum pounded his gavel and cried, "The meeting will now come to order!" When everyone had quieted down, the mayor asked, "Does anybody have any suggestion to make about our Christmas celebration?"

Mrs. Jump-Bunny jumped to her feet. "I suggest that we have a Christmas party, like we had last year," she said.

"But we *always* have a Christmas party," Miss Chipmunk objected. "Couldn't we do something *different*?"

"What's the matter with parties?" grumbled the others.

Then Mr. Cinnamon stood up. "There is a Home for Aged

45

Animals in Stumptown," he said. "I suggest that we go over there and entertain the old folks on Christmas Eve."

"Why that's a lovely idea, Mr. Cinnamon!" everyone cried.

Mr. Cinnamon smiled and sat down. He was delighted that the others had liked his idea.

Then the animals began to plan the program. Mr. Groundhog volunteered to play Christmas music on his fiddle. Miss Chipmunk said she would give a recitation. Granny Fox offered to sing "The Cozy Hollow Christmas Carol." Mrs. Possum said that her little Flossie would dance a fairy ballet. Others also volunteered to take part in the program.

Then Mr. Cinnamon asked, "May I be in it, too?"

A hush fell over Hoppity Hall. Everyone was thinking that Mr. Cinnamon might make a lot of mistakes and spoil the program. "What can you do, Mr. Cinnamon?" asked Miss Chipmunk.

"Well, I don't know yet," the bear replied. "But I'm sure I'll discover some talent in myself before Christmas Eve."

The animals sighed and wondered what to do about Mr. Cinnamon. Then Mr. Poke-Turtle remarked, "The Christmas entertainment was Mr. Cinnamon's idea, so I think he should be in it." No one said anything to the contrary, so the bear's name was added to the list of performers.

After the meeting, Mr. Cinnamon went home to bed. He hardly slept a wink for worrying about the Christmas entertainment. "Dear me," he thought, "here I am on the program, and I'm not even sure that I have talent!" All night long he kept hopping out of bed to see if he had any talent. He tried jigging around the bedroom, but decided he was too clumsy to be a dancer. He experimented with singing, but

46

discovered that he could not sing any high notes. And he couldn't remember the words to a single recitation. At last he gave up and dropped off into an uneasy slumber.

Then the next morning Mr. Cinnamon thought of something! He remembered that he had a book called *How to Become a Marvelous Magician*. He scampered into the living room and found the book on his bookshelf. "My worries are over!" he cried. "I'll be a *magician* on Christmas Eve!"

During the next few weeks, Mr. Cinnamon studied and practiced magic tricks. Much to his concern, he couldn't seem to do the tricks properly; he was always fumbling and dropping things. Objects that were supposed to pop out of his sleeve popped out of his pants leg instead. It was all very discouraging and confusing. "Oh well," he thought hopefully, "I'm sure that everything will turn out all right on the night of the show."

On the last few days before Christmas, Mr. Cinnamon worked very hard to get his act organized. He jotted down a list of the tricks he would do. There was one exciting stunt he wished to use as an ending to his act. It was called "Pulling a Rabbit out of a Hat."

Mr. Cinnamon,

however, decided against using a rabbit. He felt that a rabbit would not be Christmasy enough. Also, he was certain that none of the rabbits in Cozy Hollow would consent to being pulled out of a hat. So he decided that he would pull a Christmas plum pudding out of his hat instead.

He studied the book to see how the trick was done. It required a lot of skill and swift, clever movements of the paws. "I'll simplify this stunt," he thought. "I'll just put the plum pudding inside the hat *before* my act begins, and I won't let the audience see that it is there. Then, when the time comes, all I'll need to do is reach in and pull the pudding out." He was very pleased with himself for thinking of such an easy way to do the trick.

On the day before Christmas Eve, Mr. Cinnamon made a nice, round, chewy plum pudding. He tucked it inside a magician's tall, black hat that he had bought for the show. Then he collected all the other objects he would use in his act. "There," he said, "I'm all ready for tomorrow night!"

Early on Christmas Eve, the animals met at Hoppity Hall. It was about a mile's walk to Stumptown, and they all started off together. Doctor Raccoon and Mayor Possum carried a small Christmas tree between them. The tree was gaily trimmed with cranberries and popcorn and would soon decorate the stage at the Home for Aged Animals. Mr. Poke-Turtle drove along in his Turtlemobile, with Granny Fox in the sidecar. Mr. Cinnamon puffed and panted as he walked, because his arms were loaded down with his magician's equipment. The children were full of laughter and excitement. They skipped along under the bright, starry sky and sang Christmas carols all the way over to Stumptown.

48

At last the Cozy Hollow folks reached the Home for Aged Animals. Mayor Possum rapped on the front door. Soon the door was opened by Nurse Squirrel, who took care of the elderly animals.

"Good evening," said Mayor Possum. "We have come here to put on a Christmas program for the old folks."

"How kind of you! That's lovely!" exclaimed Nurse Squirrel. "I'm sure that the old folks will be tickled to pieces!" Then she led them all into a big room with a stage in it.

Mayor Possum and Doctor Raccoon put the Christmas tree on the stage while the others arranged pine benches.

When everything was ready, Nurse Squirrel asked the aged animals to come into the room. Some hobbled in on canes. There were two elderly beavers riding in wheelchairs. One aged lady woodchuck had an ear trumpet, because she was

hard of hearing. All of the aged animals looked very happy now that they had a Christmas treat in store for them.

Mrs. Possum passed out programs. Mr. Cinnamon saw his name at the bottom of the program. His act would be the last one. He took a seat behind Mrs. Jump-Bunny, then

50

set his magician's equipment in the aisle beside him.

Pretty soon the lights dimmed, and Mayor Possum announced that the show would begin.

The first act was Mr. Groundhog and his fiddle. Mr. Groundhog waddled up to the stage. Merrily tapping his foot, he played "Jolly, Jolly Christmas Holly," and "Heigh-ho, the Mistletoe." When he was through, the old folks clapped and whistled to show their appreciation.

"My, this is a good show!" thought Mr. Cinnamon, easing back in his seat. "But I'm awfully hungry from that long walk over here. I wish I had something to eat." Suddenly he remembered the plum pudding in his hat. "I'll eat just *one* little piece of it," he promised himself. "That won't make any difference to my act." So he reached into his magician's hat, broke off a piece of pudding, and gobbled it down.

Then Miss Chipmunk began to recite a funny poem called "The Frog in the Yuletide Log." Everyone laughed and clapped until she recited it once more.

Later, when Granny Fox was singing "The Cozy Hollow Christmas Carol," Mr. Cinnamon felt hungry again. Without realizing what he was doing, he kept breaking off pieces of pudding all during Granny's song. He also nibbled plum pudding while Flossie Possum danced her fairy ballet. By the time Flossie's act was over, the pudding was gone! But Mr. Cinnamon wasn't aware of this. He only remembered eating the first piece!

Now it was time for Mr. Cinnamon's magic act. The bear gathered his equipment together and bounced cheerfully up on the stage. He placed his things on a small table. Then he tossed a long, black magician's cape over his shoulders.

51

"Good evening, ladies and gentlemen," said Mr. Cinnamon with a courtly bow. "Tonight I will show you some of my marvelous magic tricks!"

First, the bear held up an egg. "I will now make this egg disappear into thin air!" he announced. Then Mr. Cinnamon waved a wand and tossed the egg toward the ceiling. But instead of disappearing into thin air, the egg plummeted down and smashed on Mr. Cinnamon's head! "Oh dear," he thought, as he wiped away the egg with his handkerchief, "I hope the audience didn't notice that mistake!"

Of course, they *did* notice. Mrs. Possum whispered to Mrs. Jump-Bunny, "Well, that's Mr. Cinnamon for you! Wouldn't you know that he would break that egg!"

Mrs. Jump-Bunny giggled. "I guess we should be thankful that it smashed on *his* head instead of *ours!*"

As Mr. Cinnamon continued, each trick turned out worse than the one before it. When he tried to pull peanuts out of his ears, the peanuts came tumbling out of his pockets. When he tried to flip a deck of cards over his shoulder, the cards went flying out into the audience. Once he poured apple juice into a bottomless cup. A wave of the wand was supposed to keep the apple juice inside the cup. But no amount of Mr. Cinnamon's magic could keep the juice from spilling all over the floor. All this time he could hear the audience tittering with amusement.

"Oh my," thought the shamefaced bear. "What a miserable, mixed-up magician I am! I'd better pull the plum pudding out of my hat right now. That's one trick that can't possibly fail."

Mr. Cinnamon picked up the tall, black magician's hat from

52

the table. He flourished his cape, waved his magic wand, and shouted, "I will now pull a plum pudding out of my hat!" He reached into his hat for the pudding. Of course, the hat was as empty as a hollow stump. Then he suddenly realized that he had eaten all of the pudding during the show!

Mr. Cinnamon blushed and hung his head. "I'm sorry," he apologized. "I *ate* the plum pudding, every last crumb of it!" As he scampered off the stage, he was too ashamed and upset to notice how loudly everyone was cheering.

Then all the folks gathered together for refreshments. The Cozy Hollow ladies had brought jars of cranberry punch and baskets of Christmas cookies.

The aged animals began to praise the entertainers.

"You were very funny, Mr. Cinnamon," chuckled an elderly beaver. "We think you're so clever the way you can make your magic tricks look like mistakes. That takes real *skill!*"

The bear blinked with surprise. "Why, these folks believe that I made all those mistakes on *purpose!*" he thought. He was about to tell them that his mix-ups were real ones when Mayor Possum nudged him in the ribs.

"No need to confess your mistakes, Mr. Cinnamon," the Mayor whispered. "The folks really enjoyed your act, and that's all that matters."

Then Mayor Possum said to the old folks, "Mr. Cinnamon is one of Cozy Hollow's most outstanding citizens. He's an inventor, and he always has clever ideas. It was his idea that we put on this Christmas program tonight."

"Thank you for your thoughtfulness, Mr. Cinnamon!" cried the aged animals. "We have had a very pleasant time!"

Mr. Cinnamon's eyes sparkled with joy. He was glad that his act had been successful after all, and he was pleased about the nice things Mayor Possum had said. But above all, he was delighted to see the old folks so happy. His great, warm heart throbbed with love and goodwill.

Just then, Mrs. Jump-Bunny handed him a glass of cranberry punch. Mr. Cinnamon took a hearty swallow and smacked his lips. "Merry Christmas, everybody!" he cried. "Merry Christmas!"

"Merry Christmas, Mr. Cinnamon!" everyone answered.

Mr. Cinnamon's
Snowy-Day Inventions

ne winter morning the Cozy Hollow streets were piled high with snow. It was the first big snowfall of the season. All of the animal folks wanted Mr. Cinnamon to shovel paths for them, but they couldn't find him anywhere. They gathered at the village store, hoping to find him there.

"A fine odd-job bear he is!" grumbled Mayor Possum. "Just when we need him to do odd jobs for us, he disappears!"

Presently, some of the village children came rushing up from the direction of Frog Puddle Pond.

"We found Mr. Cinnamon at Frog Puddle Pond!" Potpie

Groundhog exclaimed. "He's ice skating on *wheels*!"

"What's more, he's *sitting down* while he's ice skating!" squealed Flossie Possum. "Oh, he looks so funny!"

"Heavens!" groaned Doctor Raccoon. "It sounds like another one of Mr. Cinnamon's inventions! Let's hope that nothing goes wrong!"

Then everyone hurried to Frog Puddle Pond, where they found Mr. Cinnamon skimming around on the ice. He was riding something that looked just like a two-wheeled bicycle. However, the wheels did not have tires on them. They were as thin and sharp as ice-skate blades.

"Howdy, folks!" called Mr. Cinnamon. "How do you like my *Ice-bike*? It's one of my snowy-day inventions. I invented it for folks who like to sit down while they ice skate!" Then the bear began to pump the Ice-bike's pedals.

"Humph! It seems to me it would be easier to *skate* than to pump those pedals," remarked Granny Fox.

"He's not pushing the pedals now!" cried Jimmy Jump-Bunny. "Whee! Look at him go! He's on his fourth time around the pond, and he hasn't moved a muscle!"

But no one noticed the deep, sharp groove that the Ice-bike wheels had cut into the ice. For more than an hour, Mr. Cinnamon had been riding around in the same wide circle instead of branching off onto other routes.

Suddenly there was a loud CRACK! The ice in the center of the pond drifted away from the edges. Mr. Cinnamon's Ice-bike wheels had cut an island right in the middle of the pond! As the edges dropped away, the island sank, and Mr. Cinnamon sank with it!

"Help!" cried the bear. "Help!"

56

Quickly Mayor Possum and Doctor Raccoon jumped into the pond after Mr. Cinnamon. It wasn't until they were soggy and wet that they remembered Frog Puddle Pond was only two feet deep! Sputtering with indignation, the two animals hauled Mr. Cinnamon and his Ice-bike to shore.

"Oh thank you!" puffed the bear. "You saved my life!"

"Nonsense!" growled Doctor Raccoon. "If you had looked before you shouted, you would have discovered that the water was hardly deep enough to wet your big toe!"

"AHCHOO!" sneezed the shivering Mayor Possum. "Why didn't you stay home and shovel our walks instead of getting us all into trouble with that silly Ice-bike?"

"Boo-hoo! The pond is ruined for ice skating, too," sobbed Flossie Possum. "There's nothing left but the edges!"

Mr. Cinnamon felt very bad about the trouble he had caused. To make amends he told the animals that he would shovel their streets and walks free of charge. And he promised the children he would help them build a snow house when his work was done.

Everyone forgave Mr. Cinnamon, and they all walked back

to the village. Mr. Cinnamon said that he would clear away the snow as soon as he had had a bite of lunch.

Right after lunch the Cozy Hollow folks heard a loud rumbly-bumbly noise in the street. They rushed out to their porches, then stared in amazement. Mr. Cinnamon was riding up Main Street in an *easy chair*! He had on his horn-rimmed spectacles and was busily reading a copy of *The Jolly Journal for Animals*. There were sled runners on the bottom of the easy chair, and down in front of the runners, a big, wide snow shovel was attached. While a motor drove the chair along, the shovel plowed a path in the street!

"Howdy, everybody!" called the bear. "How do you like my *Shovel-chair*? It's a dandy invention for those who like to sit down while they shovel snow!"

"For goodness' sake!" cried Mrs. Possum. "You ice skate sitting down, and you shovel snow sitting down. Why do you have to do everything *sitting down*?"

"It's restful," he replied. "Besides, it's fun to read *The Jolly Journal for Animals* while I'm shoveling snow."

Then the bear chugged on down Main Street. When he had

finished plowing the street, he turned the steering lever and began shoveling the sidewalks.

The animals watched him to make sure that nothing went wrong. But, for once, an invention of Mr. Cinnamon's seemed to be working perfectly.

The last walk to be plowed was Granny Fox's. When the bear reached Granny's house, she said to him, "Would you mind if I rode along with you, Mr. Cinnamon? That Shovel-chair looks like fun!"

"I'd be delighted to have your company," he said.

Mr. Cinnamon put down his magazine. Then he stopped the motor so that Granny could squeeze into the seat beside him. They drove off, laughing and chatting together.

But alas, Mr. Cinnamon became so interested in the conversation that he forgot to keep his eye on the path. The Shovel-chair hit a big stone!

The stone crashed against the motor, then banged the steering lever. Suddenly, the Shovel-chair went zooming across the yard like a rocket!

"Help! Slow down!" Granny shrieked.

"I can't!" shouted Mr. Cinnamon. "The Shovel-chair is on the blink! It won't stop, steer, or slow down!"

"Oh dear!" cried Granny, holding on to her pink earmuffs. "Now what shall we do?"

"The motor runs on sassafras oil," said Mr. Cinnamon. "We'll just have to wait until the Shovel-chair runs out of sassafras oil!"

Now the Shovel-chair was crazily zigzagging all over Cozy Hollow. It plowed up Mrs. Jump-Bunny's front lawn. Then it cut a path through Miss Chipmunk's backyard. The snow whirled in all directions like a wintry white tornado. The other animals tried to rescue them, but the Shovel-chair was too speedy.

All at once Mr. Cinnamon and Granny went whizzing up Quackenbush Hill. The chair reeled around and came trundling down again. Then, ZIP! Up it went again! It whizzed up and down the hill five times!

"Heaven help us!" cried Granny. "I feel like a rubber ball! Oh, when will we ever run out of sassafras oil!"

"Have courage, Granny!" shouted Mr. Cinnamon. "We're bound to run out of it soon!"

Just then they *did* run out of sassafras oil. They stopped so quickly that they sailed headfirst into a snowbank!

Pretty soon, all the Cozy Hollow animals were busy hauling Mr. Cinnamon and Granny Fox out of the snow.

"Are you all right?" asked Doctor Raccoon.

"I'm fine," puffed Mr. Cinnamon, digging snow out of his ears. "How's poor old Granny?"

Granny was brushing an icicle from her nose. "Poor old Granny, fiddlesticks!" she snapped. "I'm fine, too. I'm not so old that I can't enjoy a nice, peppy ride in a Shovel-chair!"

Granny was such a good sport about it all that the others began to laugh.

"Oh my," said Mrs. Jump-Bunny as she chuckled. "Mr. Cinnamon certainly has made Cozy Hollow an exciting place to live!"

"Come, Mr. Cinnamon," Flossie Possum cried then, "you promised us children that you would help us build a snow house!"

Feeling very happy that no one was angry with him, Mr. Cinnamon skipped off with the children. The little Raccoon twins, Rosie and Roxie, suggested that they build the snow house behind Hoppity Hall.

"Let's build a round igloo," said Potpie Groundhog. "That's the kind of house that Eskimo animals live in."

"Wait until I go get another snowy-day invention of mine," said Mr. Cinnamon.

He hurried over to Gingerbread Cottage. Soon he returned with a big, flat wooden paddle. "This is a *Packing-paddle*," he told the children. "You paddle snow with it, and it makes the snow as hard as ice. It's just what we need to make nice, solid snow-bricks for our igloo."

The children and the bear began to build their igloo. First, they molded big, square bricks out of the snow. Next, they paddled the bricks with the Packing-paddle until the snow-bricks were very hard. Then they piled the bricks one on top of another.

"This Packing-paddle really works fine, Mr. Cinnamon," said Potpie Groundhog. "The snow-bricks are so hard they won't melt for weeks and weeks!"

61

Pretty soon Mr. Cinnamon began to feel sleepy, and he just longed to take a nap. "I think I'll sit down and rest for a while," he said.

"Ho, ho!" laughed Flossie Possum. "Mr. Cinnamon likes to *sit down* when he builds snow houses, too!"

Mr. Cinnamon plopped down and leaned wearily against the wall of snow-bricks. Then he promptly fell asleep.

The children built the igloo right around him. After a time, the igloo was all finished, with Mr. Cinnamon snoring away inside.

"We almost forgot the tunnel," said Roxie Raccoon. "All igloos have tunnels."

Then the children made some more bricks with the Packing-paddle and built a tunnel in front of the igloo door. "Mr. Cinnamon!" shouted the children. "Come out and see our Eskimo house! It's all done!"

Inside the igloo, Mr. Cinnamon awoke and blinked his eyes. It was almost evening now. The light coming through the small tunnel shaft was shadowy and dim. The bear poked his head through the tunnel opening. But that was as far as he could go! The rest of him was too round and plump!

"Yoo-hoo!" Mr. Cinnamon called to the children. "You'll have to knock down the igloo. I'm afraid I'm stuck inside here!"

The children pounded at the snow-bricks. Pretty soon they cried, "We can't knock it down! The Packing-paddle made the snow-bricks too solid!"

Mr. Cinnamon groaned with despair, "You'd better ask your parents to come chop me out of here!"

The children scampered away to get some help. Soon they

62

returned with a crowd of grown-ups, carrying hatchets.

"Have patience, Mr. Cinnamon!" shouted Mayor Possum. "We'll have you out of there in two shakes of a squirrel's tail!"

The animals began to chop the igloo. But their hatchets didn't make the slightest dent in the snow-bricks!

By this time, a large crowd had gathered around.

"What shall we do?" asked Mayor Possum. "We just can't break this house down."

"Boo-hoo!" sobbed Flossie Possum. "Poor Mr. Cinnamon will be stuck in the igloo all winter!"

Just then Miss Chipmunk spoke up. "I have an idea! Let's build bonfires around the igloo. The heat of the fire will melt the snow!"

"A splendid idea!" said Mr. Groundhog at once. "I'll

donate marshmallows and weenies from the village store. Then we can all have a weenie roast over the bonfires!"

Soon the animals had three huge bonfires roaring around the igloo. The bright, dancing flames put everyone into a gay and festive mood. They toasted their marshmallows and weenies, sang songs, and had a wonderful time. The children kept carrying snacks to Mr. Cinnamon so that the bear wouldn't feel left out of things.

After a while the igloo melted, and Mr. Cinnamon was able to dig his way out. "Oh dear," he said, stretching his stiff legs, "if only we hadn't used my Packing-paddle to make the snow-bricks, this never would have happened. I'm sorry I caused so much trouble."

"Why, you didn't cause any trouble!" laughed the animals. "You simply caused a *surprise weenie roast*. And that's a perfect way to end a nice, snowy day!"

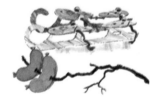

Mr. Cinnamon's Spring Tonic

inter was over and spring had come to Cozy Hollow. The village began to hum with activity. All of the animals were busy spring cleaning, repairing their houses, and sprucing up their yards. Naturally, an odd-job bear was in great demand.

One morning Mr. Cinnamon rolled out of bed, feeling very lazy and light-headed. He glanced at the list of odd jobs he had to do that day. The list said:

Wash Mrs. Jump-Bunny's downstairs windows.
Fix Mayor Possum's leaky roof.
Cut Granny Fox's grass.
Beat Miss Chipmunk's parlor rug.

"Oh my," yawned the bear, "it tires me, just to think about all that work. What I wouldn't give to spend a restful day, fishing at Bluegill Brook!" Sleepily Mr. Cinnamon wriggled into his overalls. He ate a lazy bear's breakfast of cold, left-over mush. Then he picked up a tin bucket and strolled over to Mrs. Jump-Bunny's house.

Mrs. Jump-Bunny was out in the yard, airing her winter woolens on the clothesline. "Well," she remarked, "you're late this morning. I was wondering if you had forgotten about my windows."

"No, I didn't forget," sighed Mr. Cinnamon. "I just feel very lazy today, and it takes me a long time to get around."

"Humph!" said Mrs. Jump-Bunny, eyeing him closely. "You've got a case of spring fever, if you ask me."

"Maybe so," yawned the bear. Then he filled his bucket with water and he began washing the kitchen windows.

Mr. Cinnamon worked as fast as he could, until Mrs. Jump-Bunny went into the house. Then the bear worked slower and slower. At last, he wasn't working at all. "My oh my oh my," he groaned, "I'm just too weary to move

another muscle. Perhaps, if I spent a few hours at Bluegill Brook, I'd feel like working again."

He emptied his bucket and carried it back to Gingerbread Cottage. Then he picked up his fishing rod and a can marked "worms" and ambled off to Bluegill Brook. There he baited his hook and tossed it into the water. Mr. Cinnamon lay down on the sunny bank. Soon he was snoring like a buzz saw.

It was late afternoon before the bear woke up again. A lot of Cozy Hollow folks were standing around him, talking in loud, cross voices. Mr. Cinnamon sat up and rubbed his sleepy eyes.

"A fine thing!" Mrs. Jump-Bunny scolded him. "I thought you were washing my windows. After hours of hunting around for you, I find you snoozing here at Bluegill Brook!"

"You were supposed to cut my grass today, too!" cried Granny Fox.

"And beat my parlor rug!" said Miss Chipmunk.

"And fix my leaky roof!" growled Mayor Possum. "Really, Mr. Cinnamon, no self-respecting bear should lie down on the job like this!"

Mr. Cinnamon hung his head. "I'm sorry," he apologized. "I just feel too lazy to work today."

"I think he has spring fever," claimed Mrs. Jump-Bunny. "I thought so this morning, and I still think so."

"No doubt about it," nodded Granny Fox. "You need a *spring tonic*, Mr. Cinnamon. You go right home and take two spoonfuls of sulphur and molasses. By tomorrow, you'll be feeling as peppy as a woodpecker pecking a pine tree."

After the others had left, Mr. Cinnamon stayed beside the brook for awhile. "Ugh," thought the bear. "I hate sulphur and molasses! There must be something else I can take that will make me feel just as peppy."

While he sat there thinking, he noticed that the ground around Bluegill Brook was thick with green herbs and juicy little roots. "I have an idea!" he cried. "Natural herbs and roots are supposed to make splendid tonics! I'll gather some of these and invent a spring tonic of my own!"

Mr. Cinnamon collected a quantity of herbs and roots and carried them home in his hat. Then he put the herbs and roots into his soup kettle and boiled them on the stove. To give it flavor he poured in some purple grape juice he had bottled last autumn. He ate his supper while he waited for the tonic to cool. Then, just before he hopped into bed, he drank a tall glass full of his spring tonic. It was light purple in color and very tasty. "Delicious!" sighed Mr. Cinnamon. "I'll name it *Purple-herbal punch!*"

About midnight, Mr. Cinnamon suddenly sat up in bed. He began to chuckle and bounce up and down on the mattress. "Oh my!" he crowed. "I'm just bursting with good health and energy. That punch of mine surely has made a new bear of me! I can't wait to get started on that list of odd jobs!"

When he saw by the clock that it was only midnight, he snuggled down in his pillow and tried to go back to sleep. But his toes wiggled, his knees jerked, and his paws twitched restlessly upon the coverlet. "Oh dear," thought the bear, "my muscles are having a terrible tussle with themselves. I'll just have to get up and work off some of this excess energy."

Mr. Cinnamon bounced out of bed and hopped into his overalls. He put on his *Night-light hat*, a hat he had invented to wear on evening strolls. On the brim of the hat was a small

68

lantern which cast a bright glow all around him.

Then Mr. Cinnamon poured some water into his bucket, and pranced off to Mrs. Jump-Bunny's house. Whistling cheerily, he began to wash her windows. As he polished the glass panes, the polishing cloth made shrill squeaky noises.

After awhile Mrs. Jump-Bunny poked her head out of an upstairs window. She saw Mr. Cinnamon's Night-light hat bobbing about in the darkness. "Is that *you*, Mr. Cinnamon?" she whispered hoarsely. "What are you doing down there at one o'clock in the morning?"

"I've just finished washing your downstairs windows!" Mr. Cinnamon replied happily. "You ought to jump back in bed now, my dear. Pleasant dreams!"

Mrs. Jump-Bunny jumped back in bed. "Pleasant dreams, indeed! That foolish bear has me *wide awake*!"

Now Mr. Cinnamon hustled back to Gingerbread Cottage for his lawn mower. Soon he was racing up and down Granny Fox's lawn. The lawn mower went SNIPPITY-CHUG, SNIP, SNIP-SNIP! Pretty soon Granny Fox leaned out of her bedroom window. "What's all that snipping and chugging out there?" she cried.

"It's me, Mr. Cinnamon," called the bear. "I've just cut your grass! Goodnight, Granny. Sleep tight."

Granny hobbled back to bed. "Sleep tight, fiddlesticks!" she grunted, blinking her wide-awake eyes. "Why is that bear mowing lawns at this time of night? Only a few hours ago he was too lazy to lift a paw."

Now Mr. Cinnamon was tip-toeing into Miss Chipmunk's parlor. He carried her parlor rug out to the front lawn and began to pound it with his carpet-beater. THUMP-THUD.

70

THUMP-THUD, THUMP-THUD!

Presently Miss Chipmunk raised her bedroom window. "What's going on? Are we having an earthquake?" she squealed.

"It's only *me*," Mr. Cinnamon reassured the teacher.

"It's only *I*," Miss Chipmunk corrected him.

"It's only I," Mr. Cinnamon repeated. "You'll be surprised to hear that your parlor rug has been beaten until it's as clean as a new spring lily pad!"

Miss Chipmunk mumbled something that sounded like, "Silly bear!" Then she slammed down her window.

Mr. Cinnamon felt so healthy and vigorous that it never occurred to him that he might be annoying anyone. He went whizzing off to Gingerbread Cottage for his tool kit and ladder. Soon he was skittering up the ladder to the top of Mayor Possum's roof. Humming a happy tune, he began to hammer down some shingles. BOOM-BANG, BOOM-BANG, BOOM, BOOM, BANG!

In no time at all, Mayor and Mrs. Possum bounded out of their front door. When the mayor saw Mr. Cinnamon's Nightlight hat flickering up on the roof, he shouted, "What do you think you're doing, you crazy bear? If Cozy Hollow had a jail, I'd arrest you for disturbing the peace!"

"Now, now, now, don't get so excited, Mr. Mayor," the bear soothed him. "I'm doing that odd job you asked me to do. I'm fixing your leaky roof."

Mr. Cinnamon's hammering and Mayor Possum's shouting now had the entire village awake. Dressed in their night clothes and carrying lanterns, the animals flocked out into the street.

When Mr. Cinnamon saw that everyone was awake, he realized what a nuisance he had been. "I'm sorry," he said, as he scrambled down the ladder. "I had no idea I was being so noisy. You all must be very provoked with me."

"We *are*," snapped Miss Chipmunk.

"I can't understand what has made you so peppy all of a sudden," said Granny Fox. "How much sulphur and molasses did you take?"

"None," the bear replied. "I took some tonic that I invented myself, Purple-herbal punch. It's made out of natural herbs, roots, and grape juice."

"Well now, that explains everything," grumbled Doctor

Raccoon. "But don't you know that *homemade* tonics are *risky*?" he added. "You might have made yourself sick!"

"But I feel wonderful!" exclaimed Mr. Cinnamon. "I feel so healthy and ambitious I could work all night long."

"Well, the rest of us don't feel ambitious. We're sleepy," growled Mayor Possum. "To make sure we aren't disturbed on future nights, I insist that you throw away that Purple-herbal punch, Mr. Cinnamon. It's entirely too powerful."

"But if I throw it away, I'll get spring fever again!" cried the bear. "Then how will I get my odd jobs done?"

"Well, you'll get over spring fever sooner or later," said Doctor Raccoon. "At any rate, we'd much rather have an odd-job bear with spring fever, than an odd-job bear full of Purple-herbal punch."

"All right," sighed Mr. Cinnamon. "I'll go dump my tonic in Bluegill Brook, the first thing tomorrow morning."

Everyone went back to bed then. It was quite late when the animals got up the next day. About noon, Mr. Groundhog went over to Gingerbread Cottage to ask the bear to do an odd job for him. Mr. Cinnamon was nowhere in sight.

Then Mr. Groundhog waddled up Main Street, asking folks if they had seen Mr. Cinnamon. No one had set eyes on him since the noisy night before.

Soon the animals grew alarmed. At last Mrs. Jump-Bunny remembered something. "Mr. Cinnamon said he was going to dump his tonic in Bluegill Brook!" she reminded them. "Maybe he is there now!"

The animals hurried to Bluegill Brook. They found Mr. Cinnamon lying on the bank, sound asleep. Beside him was the soup kettle in which he had made his tonic.

"Well, I guess he dumped his spring tonic into the brook all right," snickered Granny Fox. "He has the worst case of spring fever I ever saw!"

Just then, Doctor Raccoon shouted, "Look! Look at the bluegills!" Everyone stared at the brook. There they saw dozens of bluegills wildly jumping and leaping over the surface of the water.

"The fish are full of Mr. Cinnamon's spring tonic!" hooted Mr. Groundhog. "No wonder they're so spry and frisky!"

The animals laughed so hard that Mr. Cinnamon woke up. He began to laugh at the leaping fish, too.

Then, because the jumping fish were so easy to catch with their paws, the folks were able to pack Mr. Cinnamon's soup kettle brimming full with bluegills. They carried their catch back to the village. That evening the animals had the merriest fish fry ever held in Cozy Hollow!"

"This is fun, Mr. Cinnamon," chuckled Mayor Possum, as he munched his seventh fried fish. "Your spring tonic may be too powerful for animal folk, but it sure does make excellent *fish bait*! You must cook up some more of that tonic soon."

"I will," laughed Mr. Cinnamon, patting his full tummy. "I'm just tickled pink that my Purple-herbal punch is good for *something*!"

Mr. Cinnamon
Chases the Weasel

For several weeks now, the Cozy Hollow folks had been very upset and worried. A weasel thief was on the prowl! There was no end to the trouble this thief had caused. One night he broke into the village store and took twenty cans of chicken noodle soup. Another time he stole every single potato in Granny Fox's potato patch. And no one had been able to catch the weasel because he was too sly and quick.

One day Miss Chipmunk asked Mr. Cinnamon to put a padlock on the door of the pine-log school. "We have just made some pretty costumes for our school play," the teacher explained. "I would hate to have the weasel steal them."

"So would I," Mr. Cinnamon agreed. "I'm looking forward to seeing that school play. Yes indeedy!"

That afternoon Mr. Cinnamon carried his toolbox down to the schoolhouse. He tiptoed inside and began to nail the padlock on the door.

The animal children were busy practicing for the school play. The play was called *The Happy Garden*. Each child was dressed to resemble a flower. Flossie Possum was a snapdragon. Jimmy Jump-Bunny was dressed as a Johnny-jump-up. The Raccoon twins were lady's slippers. Potpie Groundhog was a purple petunia. And there were many other kinds of flowers, too.

"My, my!" chuckled Mr. Cinnamon. "This certainly is going to be a jolly little play!"

Pretty soon the bear heard the children talking about a

crab-apple tree that they needed for their stage scenery.

"Let's chop down a *real* crab-apple tree and set it right on the stage," suggested Rosie Raccoon.

"No, that would be wasteful," said Miss Chipmunk. "Crab-apple trees are scarce here in Cozy Hollow. We had better forget about a tree and use something else for our scenery instead."

The children were disappointed. They felt that a crab-apple tree would look very charming up on the stage.

"I have an idea!" Mr. Cinnamon spoke up. "*I'll* stand on the stage and be your crab-apple tree!"

"But *you* don't *look* like a crab-apple tree, Mr. Cinnamon," said Flossie Possum.

"Well, naturally, I will wear a crab-apple-tree *costume*," he explained. "I'll make it myself!"

"Goody!" squealed the children. "May Mr. Cinnamon be our scenery, Miss Chipmunk?"

Miss Chipmunk didn't know what to say. She remembered all the mistakes that Mr. Cinnamon had made in the Christmas program. She wanted no mistakes in her school play. Still, if Mr. Cinnamon was merely going to be part of the scenery, Miss Chipmunk could see no harm in that. "All he has to do is stand still," she mumbled. "He can't make mistakes *standing still.*"

The schoolteacher turned and said, "Very well, Mr. Cinnamon, you may be our scenery. You were kind to volunteer for the job."

"Think nothing of it," he replied. "That's what odd-job bears are for."

Mr. Cinnamon was thrilled that he was going to be in the play. As he set out for home, he began to sing and whistle with delight. Pretty soon he met Doctor Raccoon. The doctor looked very disgruntled.

"That weasel broke into my office while I was out making calls," growled the doctor, "and stole all of my Band-Aids!"

"I do hope we catch that thief soon!" cried Mr. Cinnamon.

"I'd better put a padlock on your office door right now."

While the bear was nailing on the padlock, he told the doctor about the school play. "I'm going to be the scenery," he chuckled happily. "I'm going to be a crab-apple tree."

"Really, Mr. Cinnamon," grunted Doctor Raccoon. "I can't understand how you can be so excited about being a crab-apple tree when there's a thief to worry about."

"Well, I can't worry about that weasel *all* the time," said Mr. Cinnamon, "and it makes me happy to know that I can help the school play be a big success."

"Humph," the doctor remarked. "I'm not sure you will *help* the play. I'm not sure at all!"

The next few days passed rapidly, and Mr. Cinnamon spent a great deal of time making his crab-apple-tree costume.

On the afternoon of the school play, the bear arrived at Hoppity Hall a half hour ahead of time. The children were already there and scampering about the stage in their flower costumes. Miss Chipmunk was straightening Potpie Groundhog's purple petunia collar.

"Ah, there you are, Mr. Cinnamon," said the teacher. "Do you have your costume?"

78

"Yes indeed," the bear replied. "I'll put it on right now."

Mr. Cinnamon went back into the stage wings. Presently he stepped out to the stage.

"Look at Mr. Cinnamon!" squealed Flossie Possum.

The bottom part of Mr. Cinnamon looked just like a tree trunk, for he was wearing a long, black gown that covered his legs and big bear feet. In his arms he carried a number of leafy, bushy branches. The branches towered over his shoulders and hid the upper part of his body. Covering the branches were dozens of bright pink crab-apple blossoms.

"Well, well!" exclaimed Miss Chipmunk. "I never have seen a more lifelike crab-apple tree!"

Mr. Cinnamon smiled behind a cluster of blossoms. Then he took his place in the left-hand corner of the stage.

Now the audience began to arrive. Everyone in Cozy Hollow came. Mayor Possum had planned to stay home and keep an eye out for the thief. But at the last minute he changed his mind and came after all.

Pretty soon Miss Chipmunk stepped up on the stage and announced, "The students of the pine-log school will now present a play titled *The Happy Garden.*"

Slowly the curtain went up and the children began to sing:

"We're little May flowers, so happy are we.
As we merrily dance 'neath the crab-apple tree."

Then the flowers joined hands and danced around the tree.

Mr. Cinnamon stood very still, the way Miss Chipmunk had told him to do. He didn't move a branch or shake a single crab apple. "My," he thought proudly, "I make dandy

scenery, if I do say so myself!"

But as the play continued, the bear began to feel hot and uncomfortable.

It was a close, muggy day. Mr. Cinnamon's bushy costume was very warm, too. Without even realizing what he was doing, Mr. Cinnamon began to pant and puff.

Every few seconds he would say, "WHEW! WHEW!"

Soon the audience began to titter. Granny Fox tapped Mrs. Possum on the shoulder. "That's a mighty odd tree," she giggled. "Never heard a crab-apple tree say 'whew! whew!' before, did you?"

"It's not so odd when you remember that the tree is *Mr. Cinnamon*," remarked Mrs. Possum. "I do wish he would quiet down, though. He'll spoil the play!"

Miss Chipmunk was standing back in the stage wings. "Mr. Cinnamon!" she whispered angrily. "Stop that *whewing* at once!"

"I'm sorry," the bear whispered back, "but I'm terribly *warm*! I do believe I'm going to faint and topple over!"

Miss Chipmunk turned pale, thinking how awful it would be if the crab-apple tree fainted. She hurried off and opened the side door of Hoppity Hall to let in some cool breeze.

After that, Mr. Cinnamon cooled off a bit, and the play went along nicely. But soon the bear felt a draft from the side door. Suddenly, he had a very strong urge to sneeze!

"Oh my, I *mustn't* sneeze!" he thought. "A sneezing crab-apple tree would simply break up the show!"

He wiggled his nose and tried his best not to sneeze, but sneeze he did! He sneezed a series of stupendous, shattering sneezes! "AHCHOO! AHCHOO!" The crab-apple tree looked as if it had been hit by a hurricane. The branches swayed and rustled, the blossoms trembled and shook. And the little actors had to stop speaking their lines until the tree quieted down.

"That Mr. Cinnamon!" growled Doctor Raccoon to Mayor Possum. "He's ruining the play!"

Backstage, Miss Chipmunk sighed with despair. "I should never have allowed him to be the scenery," she thought. "Mr. Cinnamon causes a commotion even when he's standing still!"

The bear behind the branches blushed with embarrassment. "What a *miserable, whewing, sneezing* crab-apple tree I am!" he sighed. "I hope I don't do anything else to interrupt the show."

But already more trouble was on the way! A big honeybee flew through the side door! Now honeybees dislike bears, because bears often steal honey. The moment this bee flew into Hoppity Hall, she sensed that there was a bear nearby. Though the bear was disguised as a crab-apple tree, that didn't fool the bee a bit. She buzzed angrily up to the stage, heading straight for Mr. Cinnamon!

When Mr. Cinnamon saw the bee buzzing toward him, he forgot he was a crab-apple tree. He behaved as any normal bear would behave. Mr. Cinnamon ran! And the bee chased him around the stage! As the bear ran, he clung tightly to the branches he was holding, because he thought that the leaves would protect him from the bee's stinger.

A running crab-apple tree was a very strange sight indeed. The tree tripped over the little flowers on the stage. A snapdragon squealed. A purple petunia said, "OUCH!" And two lady's slippers slipped and fell. It was anything but a *happy* garden! No matter how fast the tree ran, it could not escape the bee.

At last the tree leaped off the stage and dashed out the side door. Then the frantic crab-apple tree went galloping up Main Street, with the honeybee bumbling about in its branches!

The audience hurried outside to see what would happen next. At the moment, they were far more interested in the flight of the crab-apple tree and the honeybee than they were in the school play.

"Well," cried Mrs. Jump-Bunny, "I must say that this is the wildest school play I ever attended!"

"Poor Miss Chipmunk," remarked Mrs. Possum. "She must be very upset with the way her play turned out!"

Just then, Mr. Groundhog shouted, "Look! There's the *weasel thief* on the steps of my village store! He's all set to break in and rob me. Let's go capture him!"

"Wait a minute!" exclaimed Mayor Possum. "The thief has just spied Mr. Cinnamon galloping up the street. He thinks that Mr. Cinnamon is a *real* crab-apple tree! Look! The thief is running away!"

Sure enough, the weasel was running off toward Quackenbush Hill as fast as he could go. He was howling with terror.

"A galloping crab-apple tree!" shrieked the weasel. "This town is *haunted*! I'll *never* come back here again!"

Soon the wicked weasel had disappeared over the hill.

Meanwhile, Mr. Cinnamon had been so upset about the bee that he hadn't even seen the weasel. Then, luckily for the bear, the bee lost interest in the chase when they reached Mr. Poke-Turtle's red rosebushes. The honeybee greedily settled down for a feast of red-rose nectar!

Mr. Cinnamon dropped his branches and stumbled over to rest on the steps of the village store. Pretty soon all the other animals had gathered around him.

"Mr. Cinnamon," announced Mayor Possum, "you deserve a medal of honor for chasing that thief out of town!"

The bear looked puzzled. "I wasn't chasing a weasel," he said. "I was running away from a mad honeybee!"

"But while you ran from the bee, you also chased the weasel," chuckled the mayor. Then he told Mr. Cinnamon how the thief had mistaken him for a galloping crab-apple tree.

83

"Thanks to Mr. Cinnamon, the weasel will never come back again!" cried Granny Fox. "Three cheers for Mr. Cinnamon, our HERO!"

"HURRAH! HURRAH! HURRAH!" shouted the animals.

Mr. Cinnamon was delighted to find himself a hero. He clapped his big, furry paws and pranced with glee. But suddenly he grew very quiet. "I may have chased the weasel," he said sadly, "but I just *ruined* the school play."

"There's really no reason why we can't give the play all over again," Miss Chipmunk spoke up.

"Yes, let's give the play over again!" cried the children.

So everyone trooped back to Hoppity Hall. This time, Mr. Cinnamon was the quietest, best-behaved, crab-apple tree ever seen in Cozy Hollow!

The Fourth of July Surprise

he Fourth of July was always a big day at Cozy Hollow. This year the animals had planned a Fourth of July picnic supper in the pine-log schoolhouse yard. After supper there would be a patriotic speech by Mayor Possum. And later, everyone was going to square dance to the tunes of Mr. Groundhog's fiddle.

For several weeks now, Mr. Cinnamon had been working on a secret invention. His secret invention was a surprise for the Fourth of July. He simply couldn't wait for the day to arrive. "My, oh my!" he would chuckle to himself. "I bet my Cozy Hollow friends will remember *this* Fourth of July as long as they live!"

Finally, the big day did arrive. At six o'clock that evening the animals carried their picnic baskets down to the school-yard. The picnic tables were set with red-and-white gingham tablecloths and blue picnic plates.

"Everything looks so festive and patriotic this year!" remarked Granny Fox, as she unpacked her basket.

"Where's Mr. Cinnamon?" asked Little Potpie Groundhog. "We children want him to play Tickle the Bear with us."

Everyone looked around for Mr. Cinnamon. Just then they saw the bear bouncing across the schoolyard. He was carry-ing a little black suitcase.

"Hello, Mr. Cinnamon!" the animals cried.

"Howdy, folks!" called the bear. "Isn't this going to be a jolly affair?"

Then Mrs. Possum asked, "Where is your picnic basket?"

Mr. Cinnamon clapped a paw over his mouth. "Oh dear!" he groaned. "I forgot to bring my supper!"

Mrs. Jump-Bunny shook her head. "Mr. Cinnamon," she sighed, "you're the only animal I know who would come to a picnic supper without bringing any supper. Well, don't feel too bad. I think we all brought enough to share with you."

"Oh, thank you!" said the shamefaced bear. "I guess I forgot my supper because I was so excited about my secret invention. It's a Fourth of July surprise, and I have it right here in this little black suitcase."

The animals eyed the suitcase uneasily.

"Mr. Cinnamon," said Doctor Raccoon, "I hope this inven-tion won't cause any trouble tonight. We want no mishaps or accidents on the Fourth of July, you know."

"There won't be any trouble. It's a very jolly invention," Mr. Cinnamon declared. "I'm going to surprise you with it

86

just before Mayor Possum gives his speech."

"Very well," the mayor spoke up. "But mind, now, Mr. Cinnamon, if you do anything to spoil this happy occasion, we shall be very disappointed in you."

Just then Mrs. Jump-Bunny rang a bell. That meant it was time for supper. Everyone sat down and began to eat with a hearty, holiday appetite. The animals generously shared their food with Mr. Cinnamon.

Right after supper, the sleepy, red sun went to bed behind Quackenbush Hill. Dusk settled over Cozy Hollow. Then a silver boat of a moon drifted into the sky.

"This is just the right time of evening to show you my secret invention!" exclaimed Mr. Cinnamon. "May I?"

"Oh, all right," said Mayor Possum, "but please hurry up. I'm afraid I may forget my speech."

Then the bear opened his black suitcase. He lifted out three big, red Fourth of July rockets!

"Skyrockets!" cried Granny Fox. "Why, we haven't had any fireworks in Cozy Hollow for more than twenty years!"

"Goody! We've never seen fireworks!" shouted the children.

Mr. Cinnamon

explained, "These aren't ordinary rockets. I call them *Moving-picture rockets.* You'll understand why in a minute."

Then the bear hurried over to a wide open area. He set one of the rockets on the ground and carefully set fire to it.

The rocket began to sizzle. SSS-SWISH! It zoomed high up into the air. Then it exploded with a tremendous BANG!

The animals held their ears and shouted with glee.

The rocket had exploded into a mass of sparkling green and red stars that lighted up the sky like a thousand candles. Then gradually, the stars began to move, forming a strange-looking picture!

"Look!" said Miss Chipmunk. "It's a green dragon! It's puffing red smoke out its mouth!"

Sure enough, it was a moving picture of a jolly old dragon. The dragon began to leap around the sky, while clouds of red smoke poured from its mouth!

The children squealed with delight. Everybody agreed that it was the most unusual skyrocket he had ever seen.

"Just wait until you see the next one!" said Mr. Cinnamon, lighting his second rocket.

The second rocket sizzled and banged in the same manner. Then it exploded into an enormous, purple whale. Yellow stars were spouting from the top of its head, and it swam around high over the schoolhouse roof!

"Look at the comical whale!" the animals exclaimed. "Why are those stars popping out of his head?"

"The stars are supposed to be water," said Mr. Cinnamon. "Whales spout water from their heads, you know."

Then the bear set off the third rocket. This one exploded into a fat, blue elephant with a pink trunk! The elephant was

waving his trunk and prancing merrily over Hoppity Hall.

"That elephant is the funniest one yet!" cried Granny Fox.

Then everyone laughed and clapped and thanked the bear for his exciting Fourth of July surprise.

"They were splendid picture-rockets," Mayor Possum commented. "But when will those creatures disappear, Mr. Cinnamon? The dragon's still puffing. The whale's still spouting. The elephant's still prancing. And now it's time for *me* to make my *speech.*"

Mr. Cinnamon stared at the sky. "That's strange," he said. "Those pictures should have dissolved and disappeared long ago! But I'm sure that they will go away any minute now. Why don't you start your speech, Mayor?"

"Well, all right," the mayor replied. He cleared his throat, then started his speech. "My dear friends," he said. "My dear..."

The mayor stopped. He simply could not keep his mind on his speech. The puffing dragon, spouting whale, and prancing elephant were too distracting. Besides that, not one of the Cozy Hollow folks was paying any attention to him. They all sat gazing up at the sky, their mouths hanging open in amazement.

"Why don't those creatures go away!" said Granny Fox. "It just isn't *natural* for fireworks to behave like this!"

"Wouldn't it be embarrassing if they *never* disappeared!" remarked Mr. Jump-Bunny. "Why, Cozy Hollow would become a laughingstock. Folks in the neighboring villages would make fun of us!"

"That's true," agreed Doctor Raccoon. "We'd be the only animal village in the world with silly moving pictures leaping

90

all around us!"

Mayor Possum grew very upset. He was proud of Cozy Hollow, and he could not bear the thought of its becoming a laughingstock. "Mr. Cinnamon, we're very disappointed in you," said the mayor. "Your Moving-picture rockets have really spattered up our nice Cozy Hollow sky, and  heaven only knows when we'll be rid of them!"

Mr. Cinnamon felt very bad indeed. He realized now that he had used a few of the wrong chemicals when he had invented his rockets. However, he did have some hope to offer his friends. "I'm sure that rain will wash those pictures out of the sky," he told them. "All we have to do is wait patiently for a good, heavy shower."

"But it may not rain for weeks!" cried Mayor Possum. "All the folks in the neighboring towns will see our ridiculous-looking sky and never stop making fun of us!"

"Yes, that's so," sighed Mr. Cinnamon. "Oh, this is the most miserable mistake I have ever made! I have only one suggestion. Perhaps we can squirt the pictures out of the sky with our garden hoses."

"Well, I suppose we can try," sighed Mayor Possum.

So all the animals hurried off to their yards and turned on their garden hoses. They held the hoses up toward the sky and tried to wash away the dragon, the whale, and the elephant. But even the water from Mr. Groundhog's extra long hose could not reach the moving pictures.

Mayor Possum tugged so hard on his hose that the nozzle flew off and water spattered his best trousers. "Oh, that Mr. Cinnamon!" he sputtered. "I think I'll pass a law forbidding that bear to invent any more inventions!"

Just then the Cozy Hollow folks spied a large crowd of animals from neighboring villages. There were folks from Woodyville, Cricket Crossing, and Stumptown. They were all carrying lanterns and chattering in excitement.

"Hello there!" called the visitors. "We saw your unusual sky pictures and have come for a closer look at them!"

The Cozy Hollow folks turned off their hoses and ran to greet their neighbors. Then Mayor Possum told the visitors that the pictures would remain in the sky until rain came and washed them away. "I hope our pictures won't annoy you too much," he sighed.

Mayor Woodchuck of Woodyville said, "Why, those pictures don't bother us at all. It's a wonderful invention! Indeed, it's remarkable that the moving pictures should last so long. Do you mind if we all stay and watch them for a while?"

Mayor Possum smiled with relief. He was delighted that Cozy Hollow was being admired instead of laughed at. "Of course you're welcome to stay!" he cried. "And I'd like you to meet Mr. Cinnamon, the inventor of the Moving-picture rockets."

Then all the visitors shook Mr. Cinnamon's paw and complimented him on his invention. Mr. Cinnamon was so happy that his smile almost touched his ears.

Pretty soon Mayor Possum invited everyone down to the schoolyard to dance by the light of the moon. Then Mr. Groundhog tuned up his fiddle and began to play a piece called "The Hoppity Toad from Down the Road." As he sang, Mr. Groundhog called the dance formations.

"Come, you hoptoads, hop to your feet.
Promenade with a hoppity beat.
Grab your partner, hug her tight;
Then hop with the toad who's on your right,
Swing her high and swing her low.
Now everybody do-si-do!"

The animals hopped and danced by the light of the moon. Of course, they were also dancing by the light of the puffing dragon, the spouting whale, and the prancing elephant. And that made things even more festive.

The whole group danced until they

were all tuckered out. Then Mayor Possum gave his long-delayed Fourth of July speech. By this time, he had forgotten everything he had planned to say, so he made up a new speech.

He said: "My dear friends and neighbors, I am so glad that you could all be here tonight. Because of Mr. Cinnamon, this has been the friendliest, most neighborly Fourth of July celebration ever held in these parts. We're truly delighted that Mr. Cinnamon came to Cozy Hollow last autumn. And we hope that he stays with us for a long, long time."

"I will!" cried Mr. Cinnamon, as the Mayor took his seat. "I'm going to stay here and work at my odd jobs and inventions as long as I live. You just can't imagine all the jolly inventions I'm planning to invent in the future."

"Oh, yes we can!" laughed the Cozy Hollow folks. "We can just imagine!"

Much later that evening, the sleepy animals went home to their beds. The sliver of moon slipped quietly over Quackenbush Hill. The twinkling stars paled and disappeared. However, Mr. Cinnamon's jolly dragon, whale, and elephant remained over Cozy Hollow until the rain washed them away on the sixth of July!

About the Author

Frances B. Watts "almost fainted" when her first story was published by *Child Life* in 1956. Since that time, she has written hundreds of stories, plays, rebuses, and rhymes for children's publications. *Tales of Mr. Cinnamon* is her first full-length book. A graduate of Swarthmore College with a master's in education from Elmira College and a love for young people, she was often tempted to teach full time. Her husband, Gordon, however, insisted she only substitute in local school systems to allow her time to write. Frances and Gordon Watts live in Elmira Heights, New York, and spend their winters in Florida.

About the Illustrator

Marcia Mattingly began her art career as a set designer for the Children's Summer Theatre in Lafayette, Indiana. A degree in Design from Purdue University prepared her for subsequent employment in magazine design and illustration at The Curtis Publishing Company. Currently a free-lance artist in the Indianapolis area, Marcia enjoys hiking, boating, piano-playing, and gourmet cooking. She also finds time to teach a class in basic drawing and painting for children.

96